TEN ORANGE PUMPKINS

For Stefanie

ISBN 978-1-338-11026-5

Text and illustrations copyright © 2013 by Stephen Savage.
All rights reserved. Published by Scholastic Inc., 557 Broadway, New York, NY 10012,
by arrangement with Dial Books for Young Readers,
an imprint of Penguin Young Readers Group, a division of Penguin Random House LLC.
SCHOLASTIC and associated logos are trademarks and/or registered trademarks of Scholastic Inc.

The publisher does not have any control over and does not assume any
responsibility for author or third-party websites or their content.

12 11 10 9 8 7 6 5 4 3 2 1   16 17 18 19 20 21

Printed in the U.S.A.   40

First Scholastic printing, September 2016

Designed by Stephen Savage and Lily Malcom
Text set in Agilita Bold
The artwork for this book was created using digital and traditional media. No pumpkins were harmed in the making of this book.

Thanks to Brenda, Robin, and Wes.

TEN ORANGE PUMPKINS

PUMPKINS

A Counting Book by Stephen Savage

Ten orange pumpkins,
fresh off the vine.
Tonight will be a spooky night.

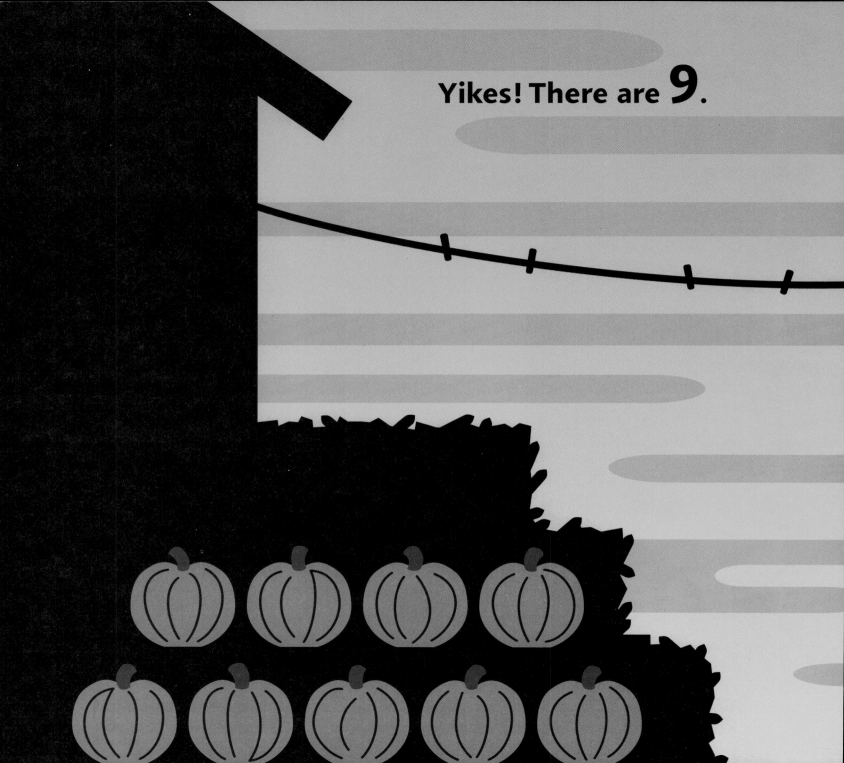

Yikes! There are 9.

Nine orange pumpkins
sit outside the gate.
Which one will the mummy choose?

Hah! There are **8**.

Eight orange pumpkins
Beneath a starry heaven.
Thunderclouds come rolling in.

Flash! There are 7.

Seven orange pumpkins
ripe for treats and tricks.
Something sweet is in the air.

Boo! There are 6.

Six orange pumpkins
out for a drive.
Watch out! There's a bump ahead.

Splash! There are 5.

Five orange pumpkins
stranded on the shore.
Yo-ho-ho! A pirate ship!

Arrr! There are **4**.

Four orange pumpkins
by an old oak tree.
Owl swoops down on
silent wings.

Whoosh! There are 3.

Three orange pumpkins.
A pot of witches' brew.
This will add a tasty touch!

Poof! There are **2**.

Two orange pumpkins.
A sticky web is spun.
Look who's crawling closer now.

Gasp! There's only **1**.

One orange pumpkin
nowhere to be seen.

Here it is,
all aglow.

Happy
Halloween!